THE
LOVER'S PATH

THE LOVER'S PATH

KRIS WALDHERR

HARRY N. ABRAMS, INC., PUBLISHERS

IN ASSOCIATION WITH

MUSEO DI PALAZZO FILOMELA ✳ VENICE

TABLE OF CONTENTS

LIFE IMPRISONS ME. I YEARN FOR FREEDOM.

A caged nightingale witnessed an angel's flight upon the lover's path. Desperate for escape, the nightingale begged the angel to free her, promising in return to love him forever. Beguiled by her song, the angel agreed and unlocked the cage. Together they flew into the heavens, the nightingale's music coaxing the angel ever higher. However, the angel did not notice as he drew too close to the sun, and his wings caught fire. Unable to save himself, he plunged into the sea. But not all was lost: the nightingale flew away, captive no more.

PRELUDE

SIXTEENTH-CENTURY VENICE WAS A RICH MELANGE of cultural influences arising from the steady interaction of intellectuals, artists, diplomats, travelers and merchants. Yet this liberal world offered women few roles to which to aspire outside of wife, mother and nun. Those able to transcend conventional boundaries succeeded only as a result of extraordinary talent, beauty or wealth.

This book was written by one such woman—a woman brave enough to let her voice resound at a time when most of her gender lived silent, restricted lives. It is dedicated to another woman, a generous and powerful patroness who had won the author's trust. And now it is offered to you.

We at the Museo di Palazzo Filomela are pleased to present this first English language publication of *The Lover's Path* (*La Via dell'Amante*), written in 1543 by the Palazzo's most noted resident, the musician Filamena Ziani.

Filamena Ziani (1510–1567) sang at a time when ensembles of professional female singers, called *concerto della donne*, would begin to gain favor at courts throughout Italy. She had the good fortune to

Detail from portrait
identified as
Filamena Ziani,
1531

live in Venice, which by the mid-sixteenth century ranked as the most important musical city in Europe. In acknowledgment of her musical gifts, Ziani was known to her contemporaries as *La Filomela*; *filomela* is the Italian poetic word for "nightingale," derived from the Latin *philomela*. In classical mythology, Philomela is the name of a princess who escaped attackers by transforming herself into a sweetly singing nightingale—an appropriate endearment for a woman who used her musical talents to escape the limitations of a world in which women had little freedom and few choices.

Ziani dedicated *The Lover's Path* to her patroness Felicita Lando, the daughter of the Doge of Venice. Sumptuary laws enacted in

Come Psiche che persegue Amor dopo che il suo dardo abbia perforato la sua anima, oso suggerire che questa che offre vi riconda di che cosa significa amare, allineare, assolutamente ed irrevokabile. Per allineare amare un altro, uno deve seguire la via del gli amante— dovunque possa prenderlo. Quello non a che cosa ave te detto me una volta?

O forse i miei testa sono come febbrile come il desiderio che vi sie te svegliati?

Se nella vita o nel sogno, prego seguite il via del gli amante ai miei braccei, in cui posso abbracciarlo con tutta la morbidezza delle piume cadute dal nido del filomela.

Letter written to Filamena Ziani, author unknown

1543 contributed to Ziani's decision to publish *The Lover's Path* in 1544. Some of these laws prohibited women who chose unconventional lives from wearing pearls and other luxury items in public, thus condemning them as prostitutes. This situation made it urgent for Ziani, as a female performer, to protect herself and her livelihood by definitively establishing her role as a respected musician in Venetian society.

Written partly in response to gossip about the author's past, *The Lover's Path* takes the form of an extended confession recounting the *fiabla*, or fairy tale, of a young woman's forbidden love. Woven within Ziani's narrative are illustrations of famous lovers, their

3

Interior spread, La Via dell'Amante, *1544*

stories serving as allegorical commentary. Because of its subject matter, *The Lover's Path* was quickly suppressed upon publication. It achieved wider recognition only in the mid-nineteenth century, when the Palazzo Filomela was opened to the public and Ziani's book, along with many of her personal artifacts, was exhibited for the first time.

Despite this temporary resurgence of interest, Ziani's name has suffered the fate of many female artists of the Italian Renaissance. She has been forgotten, and her work neglected, except by those who chance upon her former home at the Palazzo Filomela.

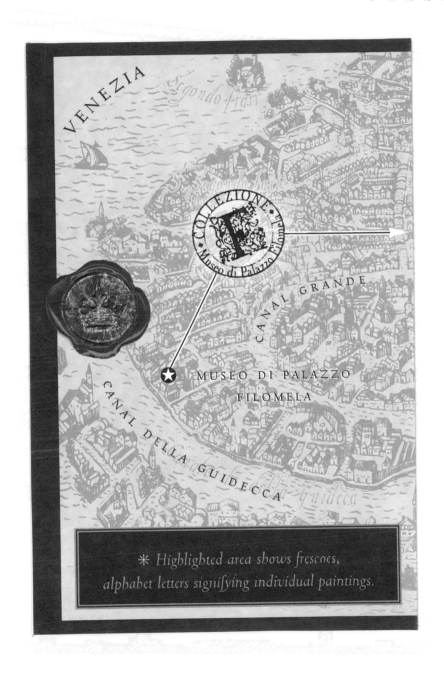

VENEZIA

COLLEZIONE · Museo di Palazzo Filomela

CANAL GRANDE

MUSEO DI PALAZZO
FILOMELA

CANAL DELLA GUIDECCA

* Highlighted area shows frescoes,
alphabet letters signifying individual paintings.

* * *

The theme of love transcends time. This has made our work of adapting *The Lover's Path* for modern audiences a relatively uncomplicated and joyful labor.

The book design for this edition was inspired by the 1544 edition. Some of the illustrations have been adapted from tarot cards in the Museo's collection, as well as from frescoes adorning the interior of the Museo di Palazzo Filomela. These illustrations replace the woodcuts used in the 1544 edition, and have been digitally restored for reproduction. Other art and text are taken from a travel journal believed to have been one of Ziani's favorite possessions. Facsimiles of letters, also owned by Ziani, are included. To make these documents accessible to all, they have been translated into English and re-created in the style of the originals. A partial museum catalog appears at the end of this volume.

It is our hope that this new edition of *The Lover's Path* will free the nightingale from her cage to sing for a new generation.

~MARINA ROSSETTI
Curator, Museo di Palazzo Filomela
October 2004

HERE BEGINS THE LOVER'S PATH

IN WHICH JOY AND SORROW

ARE JOINED AS

ONE

Dedication to
my Revered Patroness Felicita Lando
upon the occasion of her marriage on January 15, 1543
by her Loyal Musician
Filamena Ziani.

MOST ESTEEMED LADY, I OFFER YOU THIS BOOK
in honor of the gracious consideration and infinite generosity
you have shown me for these many years. I pray, modest as
my tale may be, that it expresses my gratitude for the
kindnesses you have shown me as well as my joy in your new
union. I also hope it will reveal that which I know to be true:
To truly love another, you must follow the lover's path
wherever it may take you.

la grazia

GRACE

IL·SENTIERO·VIENE·ILLUMINATO

LA·GRAZIA

DALLA·GRAZIA·D'AMORE

THE GRACE OF LOVE REVEALS THE PATH.

Beatrice was only nine years old the first time the poet Dante saw her, he slightly older. As they grew into adulthood, he often sought her out, too stricken by his love to do more than stare at her from afar. But one night as he slept, he dreamt of a garden surrounded by water. Within this garden, Amor, the fiery god of love, appeared to him holding Beatrice wrapped in a red cloak. Inspired by this vision, Dante resolved to spend the rest of his life honoring his beloved with words and poems.

HE FIABLA OF THE LOVER'S PATH begins almost two decades ago. It is the story of two sisters, alike as doves in appearance, but different as water and wine in temperament and experience.

At that time, I was a girl of sixteen. For as long as I could remember, my sister Tullia and I lived in a palazzo set in Venice, a labyrinth of a city where we heard the sea murmur its music day and night. This palazzo was furnished by my sister through her extraordinary talents. It glittered with golden mosaics, and was graced with sumptuous paintings and intricate tapestries. Within this palazzo we were aided by servants who felt affection for us. Among them were Caterina, who was Tullia's *ruffiana*—her procuress and confidant—and Caterina's daughter Laura, who was my playmate as well as my maid. And it was there in this palazzo that I bent to my sister's rule, a sapling recognizing the sun's sovereignty.

As I write of Tullia, I will try not to be too harsh. I know many have called her a mysterious beauty, cool in the use of her considerable intelligence and allure. In all honesty, my sister was as elusive to me as she was to others. Nonetheless, I hope time has bestowed upon me a measure of wisdom as I remind myself of her unavoidable influence upon me.

Tullia was my first vision in this life. My earliest memory is of her bending over to soothe me as I sobbed the inconsolable tears of childhood, her blonde hair a dazzle of light around a divinity. Unlike most children, my first word was not *madre* or *padre*; it was *sorella*, sister, in honor of Tullia. Our parents had drowned a year after my birth, leaving my sister, the elder of us by fourteen years, to raise and provide for me.

Despite her reputation as the most illustrious courtesan in Venice, Tullia shielded my eyes from the carnal nature of love; I saw little that would make a celibate blush. But she educated me in other ways, teaching me to read and write in Italian and Latin, a priceless gift bestowed upon few women, for which I am forever thankful. She also taught me the art of music, for which I showed love and aptitude. This soon won me the affectionate *soprannome*, or nickname, of *la filomela*—the nightingale.

If it was because of my sister that I had an active mind, a voice to sing, food to eat and a roof over my head, it was also because of my sister that I was made to stay inside my home after I turned twelve. Seeing that I was of an age where men might approach me

because of her profession, Tullia did not allow me to leave the palazzo unless I was dressed plainly and accompanied by an elder servant. These occasions arose less and less frequently as time passed.

No matter how much I begged for freedom, Tullia ignored my pleas. She would explain to me in patient tones that my isolation was necessary. It was her hope that in time people would see me as a woman separate from her, rather than as the sister of a courtesan. This was small consolation, for the loneliness that colored my hours felt unending. At sixteen, I was of an age when most young women had already either married and borne children, or entered a convent to do God's work. For myself, there was nothing—only an abstract promise that might be fulfilled in the future if my sister willed it. When I think of this period in my life, I give praise to music. Music helped me survive then, just as it does now.

What else do I remember about my life at that time? Sometimes when I was alone in my room, I would toss a feather from my window toward the sea. I'd watch it float away for as long as I could, imagining the countries it might reach—faraway lands I yearned to visit one day.

I also recall the brightness of gold ducats, and of my sister's hair. The insistent chatter of baby sparrows clustered about my feet as I sang inside the walled garden behind our palazzo, the precious show of sun upon my face. The spicy perfume of oranges from our garden, the briny smell of the the sea on warm summer afternoons. The starched linen of my plain brown cloak against my young skin—the cloak that hid me from others' eyes on the increasingly rare occasions when I ventured into the world. But most of all I remember the confusion of innocence, gratitude, anger and guilt that infused my emotions toward the sister I loved, yet resented.

Now as I look back, I think Tullia truly wished our *fiabla* of two sisters to stay as it was forever, to divert time like water from its path. But of course, this was impossible. To preserve my innocence, a courtesan such as my sister would have had to layer restriction upon restriction as if they were blankets upon a winter bed. While she may have thought she was protecting me from the bitter cold, my sister only made the snow outside my window look all the more enticing.

I began to think of escape.

In May of 1526, I celebrated my sixteenth birthday, still trapped within my home. Shortly after this came La Sensa, the annual celebration marking the marriage of Venice to the sea. Despite the cruel illness that had taken so many lives earlier that spring, my sister still held her annual feast.

Many thought this unseemly, but Tullia's La Sensa feast was necessary to solidify her standing and desirability. It was for this celebration that she would compose a poem praising the powers of love and set it to music; I would perform this song to the accompaniment of her lute.

I looked forward to these recitals as a prisoner yearns to glimpse the first anemones of spring from her jail window. I loved the intense study involved in mastering new music as much as I loved the transfixed attention of my sister's guests as I sang for them. While I did not otherwise participate in Tullia's entertaining—she would not allow me, for by morning's wake these celebrations often had disintegrated into private ones of a more sensual sort—after I finished singing, I would watch from the back of the musicians' gallery, set high upon the wall of the great hall. I was careful not to let the candlelight reveal me as I eagerly spied on the world forbidden to me.

But by the spring of my sixteenth year, my joy in music was tempered with steely resolution: I would use my music to free myself from my sister.

On the evening of the feast, I still remember how I sat inside my chamber, trying with little success to calm myself. A great cardinal was coming to La Sensa. I would perform for him and more than one hundred guests. He would hear me sing. Perhaps I would gain his favor, like so many musicians before me. He would champion my art, bring me to court. I would become a *virtuosa*, a great musician, and make my own way in the world. As I studied my music, I felt the weight of the hopes I dared not express aloud.

My maid, Laura, helped me dress. I braided my hair myself. As I twisted it into a knot behind my neck, a sinuous perfume curled about me. Lilies, roses, vanilla . . .

"Like two doves we are," Tullia announced softly, standing behind me as I stared at myself in the mirror. "Both light and serene."

I exhaled her perfume and looked up. The mirror reflected two golden-haired sisters with gray eyes. One wore a simple gown the color of cream, her braided hair bare of ornaments, and the other red brocade embroidered with silver thread, the full sleeves of her dress slashed with silver ribbon, her curls woven with pearls. I felt as plain as Tullia was beautiful, a sparrow next to a bird of paradise. My sister curved her long neck, so much like mine, to rest her soft cool cheek against my shoulder. She smiled at our reflections, then took my hand to lead me to the musicians' gallery.

I followed her, cold with desperation.

From my perch, I considered the celebration already underway. I stared at the cardinal, resplendent in his scarlet robes as he held court before my sister's guests. Though the hall was full, there were fewer guests than usual, no doubt because of the sickness that still lingered. Some wore large-nosed masks of gold and silver, as if they could fool death by hiding their identities. Others, their faces bared,

were less cautious. Dressed in costly silks and velvets, everyone milled about the large wood and marble table in the center of the great hall. Gracing the table were some of the voluptuous offerings for which my sister's celebrations were famed: platters of fowl and fish and bread, with rose petals arranged like a ruddy snowfall around each dish, rare fruits preserved in cordial, nuts glistening in honey, and numerous silver flasks of wine.

On cue, servants extinguished half the candles, and suddenly plunged the room into golden dusk. Everyone fell silent. Tullia rose and greeted her guests with a graceful speech. Then she looked up at me and nodded.

As she plucked the strings of her lute, my voice soared forth.

Though I sang of love, I did not think of love. Instead, I thought of the cardinal and tried to remember all that my sister had taught me: how to sing with a tremble in my throat, how to clasp my hands and tilt my head in such a way as to mimic rapture. Soon I felt the joy that music brought me, a freedom I could not find any other way at that time in my life.

As I sang, my eyes locked with the dark eyes of a young man unknown to me. He was seated next to the cardinal, his expression unreadable. Despite the dimness of the room, light clung to him. Although not the youngest of the company present, he was certainly not past twenty. He was tall and slim, his long limbs still careless with youth. Wavy hair as dark as his eyes reached the shoulder of his deep crimson doublet, framing his wide forehead like the tarnished halo surrounding an angel in a fresco. His face, while not quite handsome, expressed an intelligence far more compelling than beauty, and a yearning intensity accompanied by an anger that I knew too well in myself.

I still do not know how I shaped each note with my lips, so conscious was I of his sharp gaze. It burned me like salt water on a wound. To escape it, I turned my face toward the cardinal.

After we finished our song, Tullia bowed first to the cardinal, then to the young man.

The candles were relit. I quickly retreated into the shadows of the musicians' gallery, just as I always did. As the night wore on, I impatiently watched and listened, my sister the focus of the revelry. Eventually I saw her slender red-gowned form retreat from the great hall, followed by her maid, Caterina, and several masked admirers, each desiring a private audience. Though Tullia had retired for the evening to her private chambers, the feast would continue.

Quickly, I stole into the hallway where her cloak—the red damask cloak she always wore outside—and my brown linen one hung on hooks side by side. I took her cloak and draped it over my pale dress. It was a shade too large, its hood concealing much of my face. As long as no one looked too closely, anyone seeing this cloak would think my sister wore it—a childish act, I know, but I was still a child then in many ways.

I slipped downstairs. As I hurried around the perimeter of the great hall, I rehearsed my long-awaited plan. I would ask the

cardinal for patronage, beg him if I must. How naïve I was then, how presumptuous! I did not yet understand that patronage is granted, not petitioned for. I kept to the shadows, staying far from anyone who might know me. The room reeked with sour wine, the suffocating press of bodies. Surrounded by drunken revelers, I was sure I remained unnoticed as I approached the cardinal.

Fixated by the sight of the cardinal's brilliant red robes and already mouthing the pretty speech I had readied for him, I didn't see the lean figure emerge from a nearby column's shadow until he stood before me, blocking my way.

"Signorina," the figure said. It was the young man who had gazed at me so piercingly, the one whose eyes had forced me to turn away. Now that he was closer, I saw his stubborn chin was eased by the unexpected fullness of a generous mouth. His nose was strong but not large— just sharp enough to lend character to a face that otherwise might look too gentle.

I curtly replied, "Signore, let me pass."

The young man shook his head gravely. "I have been told that when a gift is given it should immediately be reciprocated with another."

"I do not think so. Perhaps this is a custom outside of Venice." Distractedly, I noted the gold ring upon his thumb, the gold embroidery gilding his red cuff—a wealthy man's attire. I quickly curtsyed, then rose to continue toward the cardinal.

He called out to me, his voice demanding that I stop. "I have traveled to many places—Rome, Egypt, even China. I believe it is a custom everywhere to give a gift for a gift. It would be rude not to honor this tradition."

"And what gift has been offered?" I asked, turning reluctantly. Out of the corner of my eye, I saw the cardinal rise from his seat, his courtiers bowing before him. I knew I should run to him, to address him before he left. Yet the young man's compelling gaze rooted me to the spot, daring me to stay.

"Your song." He bowed to me. "For you, Signorina."

Before I could react, he took my hand, clutched so tightly about the long folds of Tullia's cloak, and gently coaxed my fingers open. He turned my palm heavenward to place a ripe plum, almost cobalt in hue, in my hand. It looked like a large dark pearl. I could smell its fragrance, feel its cool skin. My sister's cloak suddenly felt too warm, its texture too rough against my neck. I could not breathe.

The plum fell from my hand, rolled away into the crowd. As I turned from the young man, I forgot about speaking to the cardinal and my sister's watchful eye; I felt something I could not name, a force even more powerful than my desire to escape.

I turned and ran. I ran from the great hall into the hallway, toward the door that led to the walled garden behind our palazzo. I opened it and slipped outside, my heart hammering.

Cloaked in the darkness of night, I felt safe, hidden. I breathed in the clean acidic scent of spring, felt the soft earth beneath my feet. The stars were bright, the moon a thin sickle in the deep blue sky.

Nearby, church bells struck the ninth hour of the night, their metallic clanging softened by the peaceful lapping of canal water on the other side of the garden wall.

There was a brief sliver of light from the palazzo door as it opened then closed. And the young man was before me again. Even in the darkness I could see his eyes. Though they gleamed defiantly, even then I think I detected a sorrow in their fierce depths, as if he had seen much that other men could not explain. I wondered what he saw as he looked at me—no doubt a naïve sixteen-year-old girl in a red cloak too large for her, bristling with uncertainty and rebellion.

"Filomela . . . ," he cried to me, now exuberant. "A princess who turns herself into a nightingale and escapes in the night . . ."

"That's an old *fiabla*," I retorted, injecting a courage I didn't feel into my voice. "Tell me a story I don't know."

"Very well. I will tell you of the lover's path."

"Who *are* you?" I challenged.

But he did not answer. Instead, he drew closer and took my hands. His touch was warm, welcoming—the caress of one friend to another. Then without a word of explanation, with our hands joined as one, he spun me around and around in the night garden in a strange wild dance. Seeing my surprise, he laughed in delight.

As we whirled like children, Tullia's hood slipped from my face. I felt the cool air kiss my cheeks. My braids came undone, my hair fell loose upon my shoulders. I laughed then too, overcome by an inexplicable giddy joy.

As we danced, I remembered a book I'd read that described a land to the east where streams of fire, colored like the plumes of wild parrots, shuddered from the sky in a mysterious rain. I forgot the gray stone walls surrounding me. I forgot the sea blocking my escape and my sister's relentless shadow. I saw only the stars above me, blurring into brilliant streaks of color and light.

He left me in the garden as suddenly as he had appeared. I sat alone in the darkness for some time before I remembered my sister's cloak, my missed opportunity with the cardinal. When I went to bed that night, I found that I could not sleep.

The next day, a masked figure approached my maid, Laura, when she was alone in the piazza. He gave her a carefully wrapped package, which was addressed to me.

In the privacy of my room, Laura gave the package to me. I immediately swore her to secrecy, begging her not to tell Caterina, for I knew her mother would surely tell Tullia. My hands trembled in anticipation as I broke the green wax seal to open it.

Within the pale egg of parchment rested a small book, compact enough to be hidden in the fold of a gown. Fragile from age and use, its red binding was as rippled as a weatherbeaten stone.

When I opened the book, a letter slid into my lap.

As soon as I saw the handwriting, I knew to whom it belonged. I recognized the fruit of that hand—that hand which had grasped mine in the garden—as surely as a lover senses the beloved's presence in a darkened room. His writing was not considered, like Tullia's with her carefully chosen flourishes. Instead, his words spilled onto the page, as if he had rushed to capture them with ink before they flew away, like birds startled by lightning. And in his words, I found a music different than any I'd ever heard in my sister's songs.

He also signed his name. And upon learning who he was, I understood so much about him—his anger, his fierceness, his sorrow. His life circumstances were even stranger than mine, for he was born of power to powerlessness, just as I was born of loss to loneliness.

He was the cardinal's bastard son, Angelo.

*   *   *   *

*   *   *

*

FORTUNE

LA · FORTUNA · OR · LA · FOLLIA

LA FORTUNA

SCELGA · IL · SUO · SENTIERO ·

FORTUNE OR FOLLY: CHOOSE YOUR PATH.

In a faraway land there lived a king with a daughter named Danae—a beautiful princess about whom it was foretold that her offspring would murder the king. To escape this fate, the king imprisoned his daughter in a bronze tower set on an island in the middle of the sea. There she would never marry or have children. But one day, as lonely Danae sang in her prison, a fountain of gold streamed through the tower's sole window. Within it appeared Zeus, god of all gods, who loved the princess and promised her the riches of the world. Did Danae see the fortune before her, the lover's path? Or did she count her gold coins and think of escape?

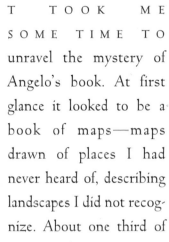

T TOOK ME SOME TIME TO unravel the mystery of Angelo's book. At first glance it looked to be a book of maps—maps drawn of places I had never heard of, describing landscapes I did not recognize. About one third of the pages were as clean as winter's first snow. Several words stamped in faded gold upon the book's spine gave the only clue to the book's contents. They read: *For Pilgrims upon the Path.*

But here I run ahead of my story—at that time I told myself that it didn't matter what Angelo offered me, what secret journeys his book might reveal. For as soon as I learned his identity, I felt an even greater desire for what his powerful father could offer me: a life of my own. The thought of this new life glittered as brightly as the gold ducats my sister accepted for her affections. It blinded my better self, eclipsing any emotions I felt that night in the garden. While I am ashamed to pen these words, I remind myself how young and desperate I was to free myself. Love seemed a luxury too expensive to consider.

Still, my heart felt heavy as I hid Angelo's book and letter under my bed, where I often stored treasures I yearned to keep secret. I sternly reminded myself who his father was, and took out paper and quill. But before I could write Angelo to ask for his help in securing the cardinal's favor, Tullia sent for me.

Within my sister's private chambers—rooms that led from the great hall through one richly appointed room after another; rooms that led to the ultimate destination of her bedchamber, where only a few suitors could hope to enter after months of courtship and substantial gifts—Tullia was being painted that day as Venus, the embodiment of profane love. Though posing was arduous and time-consuming, my sister always made an effort to encourage the attentions of artists. She knew their adoration and tributes would serve to heighten her fame and increase her fortune. It was my duty to keep her company during the tedium, to entertain her with conversation and song.

As I approached her chambers, I wondered if she had noticed that I had taken her cloak the night before. Taking a moment to ease my nerves, I stood silently in the doorway, watching.

Tullia lay on a pallet draped in the red cloak, her cat Dolce at her feet. Caterina placed a wreath of crimson roses upon her head, just as it looked in the painting already underway. Even in its unfinished state, the painting was done so skillfully that to gaze upon it was to luxuriate in the weight of the silk touching my sister's soft shoulder, the knowing luminescence of her gray eyes. But I took no pleasure in its art.

The artist adjusted a rose close to Tullia's ear, breaking off a thorn. Nodding in approval, he poured a sepia-hued pigment into an oil the color of plums, and began to paint.

Tullia was speaking to someone I could not see. "Forgive my informality," she said, her voice laced with warm indulgence. "I promised to pose, and I would not break my word, even for your esteemed company. I can converse with you as long as I do not move too much."

As soon as I entered the room, I saw a young man, dark-haired and expensively dressed, seated before my sister, just beyond the artist's view. In the brilliance of day, it took me a moment to recognize it was Angelo. This time he was clothed in somber hues, his expression serene. A small smile of either amusement or disdain—I could not tell—played upon his lips as he took in the pretty tableau of my sister's pose.

Tullia looked up to greet me, then gestured to a chair across the room, far from the reach of Angelo's eyes. Dolce jumped from Tullia's pallet as soon as I sat down. Once the cat had settled in my lap, I stroked her soft white fur to calm myself.

Angelo did not even acknowledge my presence with a nod.

A stab of jealousy pierced me, even as I reminded myself of his father's identity and how he could aid me.

"Signora, my father asked me to convey his thanks for your hospitality last night," he said to Tullia as he placed a small bag of ducats upon the table, paying for the privilege of conversation. Caterina gathered it with a deep curtsy and left the room.

"I am honored by his attention," Tullia replied. "And what of you, Signore?"

"I especially enjoyed your song."

She beamed in genuine pleasure. "I wrote the lyrics and music myself, Signore. I understand you write also. Is it true you called the pope a crocodile in one of your poems?"

Angelo shrugged, picking up a small jeweled figurine from a mahogany table to examine it. "I wrote a poem about a crocodile . . . people may think what they wish." Returning the figurine, he abruptly turned in his chair to address me. "Signorina, do you compose like your sister?"

I looked up, at once relieved and anxious to plead my case. But as I met his eyes, I was stunned to silence. I finally stammered, "I would like to—"

"My sister knows only how to sing," Tullia interrupted softly. "She is young, but soon she will be too old to perform without being judged. Then she will retire, for in the world's eyes, a *virtuosa* differs little from a courtesan. Few women may choose their fortune, but I would have a different one for her." She frowned as she shifted her weight to avoid leaning upon her elbow.

A flash of anger passed through me, but I said nothing. Instead I cast my gaze down at my hands, gently stroking Dolce. Angelo was quiet too. Dolce stretched. As the moments passed, the only sound in the room was the scraping of the artist's brush. Finally Caterina's return broke the uncomfortable silence.

"Another gift for you, Signora," she announced, offering a ribboned box to Tullia. "From Signore Matteo."

"He is persistent," Tullia commented lightly. She broke her pose to open the box, lifting up a ruby and pearl necklace. I knew how much she despised rubies, and that she would never wear this necklace; Caterina had warned her that rubies foretell a life lost too soon. Despite this, she contained her distaste to smile at Angelo, as though to say, *Desire me, for I am desired by many.*

She quickly dropped the necklace back into the box, and pulled out a gold mask. From where I sat, I could see elaborate calligraphy tracing the inside of its surface.

"Another poem," she murmured. "His riches do not buy him the muse's favor. This time he writes that since I would not see him last night, he will not wear this mask to protect himself from illness. He would tempt death for my golden hair and silver eyes . . ." She laughed, a bell-like sound. "He could be writing of my sister, for she looks like me. Wouldn't you agree, noble Signore?" She arched a delicate eyebrow at Angelo.

I strained my ears to hear his words. "Many things look the

same but are different," he replied evenly. "Water looks like spirits. Wine looks like blood . . . You are different from your sister." Then he rose and bowed stiffly to Tullia. As he left, he did not even glance at me.

Once the door closed behind him, Caterina asked, "What did he want?"

"To offer his father's compliments." Tullia waved a hand dismissively. "I was surprised to see him last night. No doubt he's returned to Venice because of his mother's death. I've heard they were close."

Caterina frowned. "He is full of righteous anger."

"Yes, I suppose he is," Tullia answered thoughtfully, as if reappraising him in a new light. "After all, consider his birth—children of his rank are only brought into this world to advance their parents' fortunes. This winter, he will marry, whether he likes it or not." And then Tullia mentioned Angelo's betrothed, the youngest daughter of a family known for their immense political power. "If he does not wed her," my sister continued, "his father will lose whatever influence he has gained in Rome."

As I listened, I averted my eyes from Tullia's. At that time of my life, my face revealed every thought that coursed through me, like currents disturbing a pond's calm surface. Despite myself, I felt the blood rush to my face as I thought of his book, remembering how the sky seemed to shatter into color as we danced.

For the remainder of the afternoon, though my sister spoke to me and I answered dutifully, I felt a gray silence within me, a disappointment I refused to name.

By the time Tullia had finished posing, hours had passed and a servant had lit the candles in her chambers against the approaching night. I was relieved to be freed of my duties and to be alone with my troubled thoughts once more. As I walked down the dark, deserted hallway toward my own room, the cool air felt like a soothing caress upon my brow.

Suddenly I felt a hand grab mine. Startled, I looked up to see Angelo, his expression intent as he led me into the shadows.

"Did you receive my book?" he whispered, his words a rush.

"Have you been waiting for me all this time?" I countered, remembering his intimate banter with my sister. Her perfume still lingered about him, insistent and voluptuous.

When Angelo nodded, it seemed as though spring had returned

after a long cold winter. But then I remembered myself. I did not waste a moment. I took a deep breath and addressed him, my tone formal.

"Signore, I would like to compose. Can your father help me?" As I said this, my voice trembled with emotion, with desperation and fear—what if he refused to help me?

Irritation crossed his face as he pulled me up from my curtsey. "If you depend on the power of others, you will have none of your own," he answered. "Is that what you really want? A life of servitude, of inconsequence in a gilded cage?"

Though his question surprised me, I steadfastly clung to my intentions, ignoring the voice of my heart. I quickly spoke of my love for music, of my sister's desire to spare me from the world's fickle nature. "But I want to write my own songs, to make my own life."

"Time and talent will reveal your songs to you. You have no need of my father for that." His expression softened at my distress. "If you want, I will speak to him. But is this all I can offer you?"

And then his eyes looked more deeply into mine. In his intense gaze, I saw frustration, rebellion and longing—and I saw myself. And in that moment, I knew I would follow him upon the lover's path wherever it might lead us.

How can one describe the first embrace of lovers? I had seen my sister kiss. I had seen men weep for her favors. Innocent as I was, there was much that I knew, more than I would have wished. I had no illusions, no romantic visions. I understood that Angelo and I

could never be together, that neither his father nor Tullia would allow it. Yet I forgot all of this as his arms encircled me. And it was at this moment that I learned that desire creates desire, for I sensed his and it gave birth to mine.

He whispered, his mouth so close to my ear I could feel the warmth of his breath, "We are kindred, Filamena. We are meant to be together."

Caterina's footsteps echoed in the hallway. I pulled away before she could see us. "I must go."

"I must see you," he whispered urgently. "When?"

The language of love is better served by music than by words, which only confuse, granting satisfaction to neither author nor reader. Now that I am older, I know too well how unsatisfying descriptions of passion are. They are like dried flowers forced to pass for fresh—only a faded skeleton remains of what once thrived. I can use words to describe how I loved Angelo, how he loved me. But they seem empty and pallid when I remember how I felt.

The next day, I waited for him in the walled garden behind our palazzo—yes, the garden where we had danced so ecstatically. No one was home except for my maid. Tullia had gone out with her servants, but I feared their return. As I paced back and forth among the herb bed, the orange tree, the ivy-laden walls, I thought of my music and of Angelo. Somehow they had become entwined within me, each granting new life to the other.

When Angelo arrived, Laura led him into the garden and withdrew.

We stared at each other. I opened my lips but no words came out, my mouth gaping wide like a fool's. As his eyes met mine, I saw the flush on his face slowly fade, and how many colors made up the darkness of his eyes, the length of his eyelashes, the new stubble on his cheeks. I noted the scar at the base of his strong chin, a wound he later told me he'd earned while swimming during a storm in defiance of his father.

Uncharacteristically shy, he looked down and took my hands. I did not pull away. I tried not to think of Tullia, of her sacrifices on my behalf. Instead, I remembered how his hands looked as he offered me that plum at La Sensa; these were the same hands that now held mine.

"I've thought only of this moment since we first met," Angelo confessed. "It has been so difficult to draw near you—you are like a princess trapped in a tower, a nightingale in a cage."

"My sister would say that she and I are like two doves, impossible to separate one from the other," I replied, with a bitterness that surprised me.

"Doves may promise loyalty, but they also promise freedom," he countered quickly.

"She would forbid me to speak to you."

"As would my father." He raised his chin. "But I don't care. Nor should you."

Silence. I heard a bumblebee gather pollen from a nearby rose.

Angelo reached up to stroke my cheek. I hesitantly touched his hair. It was soft, vibrant. Sparrows called from one side of the garden wall, seabirds from the other; their mingled songs sounded in a new music.

His voice grew tender. "I first heard you sing several weeks ago, from a boat outside the wall of your garden. I had just returned to Venice from Rome, just learned of my mother's death. There was such beauty in your voice, yet such ferocity. It spoke of everything within me that I could not express."

He paused shyly before adding, "I returned to listen to you every day after that. I came even on the days it rained. I know how ridiculous that must sound, but I *had* to know who you are. When I asked my father who lived in your palazzo, he told me it was the home of a great courtesan."

"And what of this great courtesan?" I prompted. As if possessing him with my gaze, I ran my eyes over the stubborn lines of his dark brow, the thick waves of his hair, now shining in the late afternoon sun.

He leaned close to whisper in my ear, his voice a hoarse promise, "I learned she was your sister. Then I heard you at La Sensa and I searched no more."

Looking back, I believe Angelo and I could have remained there forever, bound by each other's stares. But just then Laura rushed in. "Your sister—" she warned, her face pale with fear. I heard Tullia's musical voice as she called to Caterina, asking for me as she approached the garden.

Though he had been away for several years, Angelo proved himself a true son of Venice. He pressed something into my hand, three heavy coins. Before I could react, I heard the tearing of vines, the scattering of sparrows startled from their nest—he had climbed the garden wall and, as I watched, dove fearlessly into the canal on the other side. His body was a perfect arc of intent before I heard it slice the murky green water beyond.

Later, when I was alone, I imagined the sea caressing him as he swam, the currents swirling away from his body in neat, regular patterns. Remembering his book, I opened it for the first time since I'd hidden it beneath my bed. I examined the maps, touched the pages.

Feeling the fragile paper under my fingers, I was moved to reverently kiss an empty page. To my surprise, words emerged from the surface, as if the warmth of my breath had melted them from a prison of ice.* His handwriting challenged me:

Did Danae see the fortune before her, the lover's path?
Or did she count her gold coins and think of escape?

And so Angelo and I began to meet regularly in the garden. Now that I understood the secret of his book, we read many pages together in that hidden bower. It was also there that I sang for him, his presence infusing my voice with new passion. Miraculously, he always appeared at my palazzo door while Tullia was away. Later I learned that he waited in the piazza every day, hoping for the sight of my sister, dressed in her red cloak and accompanied by her

---

* *Editor's note:* We believe Angelo's book included examples of steganography, or the art of hiding messages with invisible inks and related techniques. Used since ancient Greece, invisible inks were often made from milk or vinegar, all of which darken when heated by an outside source.

45

servants, on the way to an appointment. He knew she would usually be gone for some hours, during which time I would be alone except for Laura, whom I had sworn to secrecy.

As spring became summer, he and I watched the walled garden turn fragrant with honeysuckle, basil and roses. The orange tree flowered, then turned green. I dared not think of what winter would bring.

It was during the week the orange tree began to bear fruit that Tullia came to me as I lay awake in my room one night.

"I want to speak with you, Filamena," she said, her dulcet voice betraying nothing. Even in the darkness, she shone. Her light hair was loose about the shoulders of her gold-colored robe. About her neck I saw a brilliant flash of red, of white—Matteo's necklace rested in the hollow of her throat like an expensive noose.

"I know this will be a surprise," my sister murmured, as she reached down to stroke my unbraided hair, just as she had when I was a small child. "I've decided we should leave Venice for the summer. Matteo has invited us to his new villa in the countryside. We leave tomorrow."

My face must have turned as still as stone, for she quickly added, "There is still too much illness here . . . I would not have you exposed to so much danger."

"You don't even care for Matteo," I protested.

"I made a promise to our mother to look after you, to protect you." Tullia paused to let her words sink in, reminding me yet again of her sacrifice. It was overwhelming. I felt as though I was drowning in her love. I began to cry; in those days, I wept as easily as a fountain.

"Shush . . ." She placed her cool hand on my brow and smiled at me. "While I was packing, I found something special. I've been wanting to give this to you for some time."

My sister placed in my hands a small portrait encased in a silver frame. The palm-sized tempera painting depicted a young woman with gold hair, eyes the color of smoked glass, an imperious nose and a long neck— a woman who looked much like me, much like Tullia.

"Our mother, painted when she was about your age," Tullia explained. "You can see by her white dress how innocent she was then, much like you. I never showed this to you because I worried it would remind you of our loss. Perhaps I was wrong." My sister cupped my face in her palms, dropping her head to meet my eyes. She looked like a lily as she bent over me.

"I remember the day she gave birth to you," she continued, gazing intently at me. "The sea surrounded you before you even drew your first breath. After she drowned, we journeyed from island

47

to island, never resting until we found our home. Water and sor-row—that is how we found our way; that is where your music comes from."

As Tullia spoke, my eyes burned with tears. Suddenly I was reminded of a morning when I was not yet four years old—not the first day I'd heard Tullia play her lute but the first time I *understood* that it was her hands conjuring those sounds from gut and wood. In wonder, I had reached for her as if trying to embrace the sun with my small hands.

"And what of our father?" I ventured.

Tullia frowned, letting her hands fall away. "I've already said too much. Sorrow shared is sorrow multiplied." She smoothed the cover-let about me, caressed my shoulder. Knowing from experience that further questioning would yield nothing, I turned my head into my pillow. Under Tullia's watchful gaze, I closed my eyes and pretended to sleep.

Several moments passed before I heard Tullia close my door behind her. Then I opened my eyes. I lit the smallest candle in my room and took out the portrait of my mother. I stared at it until exhaustion overtook me.

il desiderio

DESIRE

MI·ANNEGA·IL·MIO·DESIDERIO

IL DESIDERIO

MI·PUO·SALVARE·SOLO·IL·MIO·AMATO

I DROWN WITH DESIRE; ONLY MY BELOVED CAN SAVE ME.

When King Mark of Cornwall decided to marry, he sent his trusted knight Tristan to fetch Isolde, his Irish bride. But Isolde vowed that she would rather die than marry a man she considered her enemy—and Tristan would die too, for his loyalty to Mark. To accomplish this, Isolde mixed poisons in a cup. But she inadvertently created a potion more powerful than death; anyone tasting of it would know love beyond all bounds. As soon as they drank from the cup, Tristan and Isolde were joined together in heart and body. The lovers met as often as they could to give way to their desire, taking risks only the most foolhardy would contemplate.

THE NEXT MORNING, IT RAINED IN ONE of those sudden desperate summer storms that lasts as long as the sun preceding it. By the time the rains ceased, the canals had overflowed, flooding all of Venice for several days.

Trapped inside by water, I spent much time staring at the portrait of my mother, pondering all Tullia had confided. Emotion filled me as I thought of her story. *Water and sorrow,* she had said, *that is how we found our way.* Yet my mother did not look sad. After much consideration, I decided that her eyes, so much like mine, told another story: no matter what my sister's sacrifice, she would not have wanted Tullia to be so severe as to deprive me of happiness. She may not have wished me to be a *virtuosa* or to love someone so above my station, but gazing at that treasured portrait, I felt sure she would have understood.

In the years since, some have speculated that once Tullia gave me that portrait of my mother, I ran away from Angelo and back into her arms, like a prisoner yearning for her jail after a first taste of freedom. But they were wrong. As soon as the sea receded and the streets emerged, streaked with dark sand and small translucent fish gasping for water, I sent Laura with a message to Angelo.

I remember how I waited for her return, so uncertain of the path before me but more certain than ever of my emotions. Remembering this now, I am struck anew by the fierce convictions of youth—how little I knew of Angelo, yet how strongly I desired him! Yes, it was true I would be separated from him for only a few weeks, but that seemed an eternity.

"Where is Laura?" Tullia asked me. "It's time to leave."

I did not answer—even then I preferred silence to lies—but instead returned to looking at the portrait of my mother, which had joined Angelo's book and letter as my most precious possessions. When Laura finally appeared, breathless and upset, she confessed that she had been turned away from Angelo's door by his father's servants. Nothing could be done.

So I left Venice without seeing my beloved.

Our journey from Venice did not take long. I hated Matteo's villa at first sight, with its brightly colored frescoes and overpruned gardens, vineyards for decoration rather than wine; forests stocked with young deer for sport instead of sustenance—pretensions of honest rustic living disguising bored decadence. I despised the fine cloak of dirt that gilded my gown every time I ventured outside my small, hot room. It pained me to witness Matteo's possessive attentions to my sister, seeing how rarely he left her alone and knowing how little she cared for him. Though I tried not to think of this, it weighed on me that she had chosen to be with him to protect my life.

Most of all I missed Angelo. But fueled by memories of his tender encouragement, I used all the time I had alone to compose in secret.

I waited until everyone was away from the house, even Laura, to give way to my work. Like a bird collecting fragments of silk and parchment for a new nest, I gathered every bit of information I could remember Tullia uttering about music. I watched with new interest as she sounded out melodies on a simple wood flute; studied how she combined those notes to create emotion with sound. I recalled her comment that lutes were worthier to compose for than flutes and horns; wind instruments spoke of strife, she said, strings of harmony.

Over the weeks my ears grew sharper, my imagination quicker. Though my talents were still in their infancy, I took pleasure in their expression as well as in the hope they offered. Although I was too cautious to commit these first songs to paper, they were engraved within me, just as Angelo's words were. No matter what Tullia planned, I would be a *virtuosa*—I would be free.

During those days so green and strained only one event lightened my heart. Soon after our arrival, a messenger arrived at the villa with a package for me. It contained a flask of the finest red wine, a silver chalice, an ivory saltcellar and two white doves—the traditional gift presented upon parting by one friend to another. Tullia said nothing as she handed the basket to me. I feigned surprise and innocence, for already I knew it was from Angelo. No note was enclosed, but no words were needed—I understood his message.

We drank his wine the first night. The saltcellar disappeared into the kitchen. But the doves stayed with me. I doted upon those shy, docile creatures, feeding them morsels of bread from my hand, training them to sit side by side upon my shoulder as I strolled the vineyards in the mornings before it grew too warm.

"*La filomela* has found herself some friends," Tullia proclaimed, noting my attentions. "I know Dolce will like them too."

I begged Laura to help me find a way to thank Angelo. She reluctantly approached Matteo's huntsman, who had kindly built a small

cote for my doves. Seduced by gold, he asked no questions about the letter I pressed into his hand as he rode from the villa to the outside world. "Beloved," I wrote, "I have drunk wine from your cup. But the doves miss their master."

In reply, his letters began to arrive. Looking at his writing anew reminded me of his hands—their strength, their gentleness, how they must have handled those doves that he sent me. I imagined him touching their soft white feathers, the way they might have stretched their delicate wings in response:

Beloved

Angelo found the most imaginative ways to leave me these notes, letters charting a path that I might follow. Once I found a note wrapped in the folds of my brown cape, a bow of neat red silk tying it shut from prying eyes; I still do not know how it arrived there. Another time I found a letter tucked into a silver basket of small white peaches, the first of the season. It was fortunate only Laura was in my room when I discovered them hidden beneath my pillow.

The red book grew thicker with each new letter I hid within it, and my desire blossomed. As often as I could without attracting undue notice, I dashed out pages of quickly scrawled words, filled with simple yearning, to send to him.

In the evenings, when I sang for Tullia and Matteo, Tullia commented on how passionate my voice was becoming, chiding me only for my distracted manner.

It was several weeks after the doves' arrival that Caterina offered to amuse us by reading our cards. Surprisingly, my sister agreed to this. In truth, Tullia was a little frightened of Caterina's cards, but longed for an excuse not to accompany Matteo as he

hunted. Like me, she disliked the sight of the bloody stag sacrificed for his diversion.

Within the villa's garden, the afternoon sun bathed everything in a blinding white heat. Laura, Caterina, Tullia and I took shelter under an arbor crowned with a canopy of twisting grape leaves. These vines were jeweled by luminous green grapes no one would bother to harvest, since they were only for show. The humid air laid heavily upon us, the only sound a chorus of cicadas, their staccato chirps rising and falling in waves.

"Read for me," Tullia said, fanning herself lazily. "Distract me. You choose the cards, Caterina."

"I can already tell you your future, Signora," the *ruffiana* quickly offered. "You will be ever wise, ever desired."

"You know me too well to think I'd accept such obvious flattery," my sister teased, but I could tell she was pleased. She looked at Laura and me. "Who's next?"

"Don't do mine," Laura said, giggling nervously. "Read Filamena's fortune. Will she be famous? Will she marry?" Sensing danger, I rose to leave, gathering my doves. Torn between guilt and desire, I worried my secret would be revealed upon my face.

"Not if I can help it," Tullia answered calmly. "I wish for my sister a peaceful life. A life free of the folly of love. If she follows my will, she will be a happy woman."

As she spoke, I felt a flash of anger. To contain it, I stared wordlessly at my sister, willing my expression to remain as unreadable as hers. How mysterious she seemed at that moment—a puzzle I could never decipher, so generous yet so harsh in her love for me. Perhaps this was the allure my sister offered so many of her suitors, a cool inscrutability they yearned to thaw with their ardor.

"What is it, *filomela?*" Tullia suddenly asked. "You look so strangely at me."

"I was just thinking," I answered slowly after a moment's silence, "that my life should be mine to choose."

Caterina offered up her worn deck. "No woman can choose her life, but you can choose some cards."

I sat back down, not bothering to arrange the folds of my brown linen gown to save it from wrinkles. I grabbed the deck, shuffled the cards seven times. I spat on the earth for luck.

Caterina's usually emotionless face registered curiosity as she took the cards from my hands. She nimbly chose four from the top. "As God wills . . ." she breathed. Her hands, smooth and white even in middle age, flashed against the deep flat colors of the cards as she turned them over.

Despite myself, I felt a ripple of anticipation. I saw one card bearing silver arrows, another with golden coins and a third with a man and woman caught in an underworld of stone. A fourth card showed a couple sharing a cup, a winged heart fluttering above their heads in a cloud of fire. I flushed, remembering how Angelo and I had embraced just like the lovers on this card.

Caterina was silent, her somber brown eyes considering my future. "What do you see?" Laura pressed. "Say something, Madre."

Caterina turned from her daughter to address me. "I see many things."

I could not meet her direct gaze. "Such as?"

"Fame, both good and bad. And I see . . . a man who loves you," she pronounced.

I felt triumph yet fear at her words—yes, I would be a *virtuosa*; yes, Angelo loved me. We would find a way to be together, despite his father and my sister. It was right for me to love him, to defy my sister. I know how superstitious it must sound to put so much faith in cards and fortunes, but remember, I was only sixteen and I was desperate for reassurance.

I shook my head, careful to protect my secret. "You must mean my sister, for she is famous. It is she who loves someone."

"I'm not susceptible to that malady," Tullia said, laughing. "As soon as we return to Venice, I'll refuse to see him again."

Caterina continued. "This man wants to take Filamena on a journey to a new land."

Had she seen Angelo's book? Had Laura revealed something? Suddenly cold, I stole a look at my maid; the sun had ducked behind a grouping of tall cypress trees, silhouetting them in gold. "Maybe you speak of the journey here?" I offered weakly.

"I am only telling you what the cards say." Caterina shrugged. "If you don't want to hear it, don't ask the cards."

My hands relaxed their grip on my skirt. Perhaps Laura hadn't betrayed me after all.

"Do not accept his offer," Caterina warned, mulling over the display of brightly painted cards. "Like your sister, you have no need of his affection . . ." No doubt the *ruffiana* was only echoing Tullia's wishes. But how close her words cut!

"Go on," Laura begged. "What else do you see?"

Caterina pointed at the first card. "The six of swords. A voyage over water, a journey without end." She frowned in puzzlement. "But this card is very strange . . . This man can never marry you, Signorina, for he is trapped between worlds—"

"I don't want to hear anymore. This is silly." Shaken, I quickly gathered the cards from the *ruffiana*'s lap before she could say another word, and placed them back in their rough wooden box. Whether Laura had said something or not, I had the disturbing feeling that Caterina knew more than she had revealed. I was silent, feeling the fear of an animal who cannot see the hunter but senses he is close.

That evening I wrote to Angelo, *We are discovered.*

His response came three days later. I placed it in the red book, next to the rest of his letters.

l'inganno

DECEPTION

RESO CIECO DALL AMORE

L'INGANNATORE E RIMASTO INGANNATO

BLINDED BY LOVE, THE DECEIVER IS DECEIVED.

A prince lost in a dark wood fell in love with an enchanted swan maiden. Moved by his devotion, the unfortunate girl confided that she was cursed to remain a swan unless a virgin youth vowed to love her forever; but if this vow were broken, even by chance, she would die. The prince promised to return and claim her as his bride. The next evening a ball was held in honor of the prince's birthday. As it drew to a close, a princess arrived who looked like the swan maiden, but was as deceitful as the other was pure. Believing her to be his true love, the prince wed her, thus cursing the swan maiden forever.

VER THE YEARS, MANY HAVE wondered what could have been in that last letter to create so much sorrow. But by writing of sorrow so soon, I run ahead of my *fiabla*; I would rather relate it just as it occurred when I was so young, so ripe for joy and disappointment.

Angelo's letter to me contained no sadness, only the promise of reunion. He wrote that as soon as I returned to Venice, we would run away together. All I need do was send him a note with the date of my return and on that night, he would have a gondola waiting for me at the edge of the piazza. It would take me to an abandoned island his father owned, where no one would think to look for us. To avoid discovery, he would travel separately and meet me there. We would stay away through the winter, until the scheduled date of his wedding had passed. Eventually we would seek the blessing of a priest he knew in Rome, who would marry us in spite of the cardinal.

As for the remainder of my time at Matteo's villa, I won't write much more about those days of blistering sunlight, unmitigated by the sea's cool currents. Whether or not she had revealed my secret to Caterina, I could trust Laura no longer. I stopped composing, too distracted to concentrate on anything. My only comforts during this time were my doves and the promise contained in Angelo's letter.

As each day passed, the threat of discovery grew heavier. It weighed on me, just as my guilt and conflicting gratitude to my sister had. You can imagine my relief when Tullia announced we were to return to Venice, since the worst wave of illness seemed by then to have passed. Matteo was furious with her decision, but there was nothing he could do.

As soon as we arrived at our palazzo in Venice, I retreated to my room and shut the door. I waited anxiously for nightfall, counting the hours until I could free myself to be with my beloved. Nervously, I rummaged through my bag of belongings, searching for Angelo's journal where his letters were hidden.

The red book wasn't there.

"Laura!" I cried. Surely my maid knew where it could be; even if she had revealed my secret, she would not have stolen from me. I emptied the entire contents of the bag onto the floor—still nothing. I called yet again, desperation tingeing my voice.

Laura finally appeared. Her face was blotchy, her eyes raw with tears. "Please believe me," she sobbed, "I didn't tell them, but somehow they knew! I had no choice—"

Caterina entered my room behind her daughter. "You did have a choice—a choice to be honest," she scolded. I flinched as she slapped Laura's cheek, yanking hard at the brown curls adorning the side of her head. I had never seen Caterina hurt her daughter before. I was stunned by this display—what would Tullia do to me?

Then Caterina turned to me, her expression cold. "How could you deceive your sister?" she yelled, shaking her head.

I replied, my voice stronger than I felt, "How could you steal from me? Give me my book back."

Caterina pursed her lips and left the room for only a moment. When she returned, the red book was in her hands.

I grabbed the book from her, screaming as I ordered her and her daughter out of my room. I slammed the door, fear giving me new strength. As the door shuddered behind me, the doves took flight, their wings beating fruitlessly against the bars of their golden cage.

I slid the bolt on my door. My hands trembled as I opened the book to remove Angelo's letters . . .

Imagine biting into a ripe piece of fruit, expecting to taste sweetness, and instead finding your mouth filled with nettles. That is what I felt when I saw Tullia's handwriting instead of my beloved's—she had replaced his letters with an envelope containing one from her.

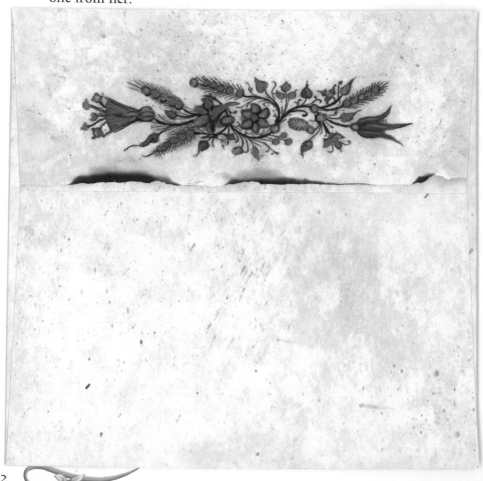

I ran out of my room, my only thought to stop Tullia. In her chamber, her trunks rested, unopened. In the hallway, her bright red cloak rested on its hook. But my brown one was missing. I ran to the musicians' gallery and looked down into the great hall. It was empty, though it was lit by candlelight as if in anticipation of company.

She was gone. I sobbed as I sank to the floor of the gallery, unable to do more than wait for her return.

It wasn't until the sky had lightened into the azure preceding dawn that I heard a door open below me. I slowly pulled myself up to peer down from my hidden perch.

Tullia was alone. She was wearing my cloak, the brown hood covering her light hair. Spying on her just as I had in earlier times, I watched in silence as she pushed the hood back. She walked about the room, dousing several of the candles on the large marble-topped table where the feast had been displayed at La Sensa, when I first met Angelo. Now only her lute and some sheets of music lay scattered upon its surface.

Suddenly she uttered, "I know you're up there." Her voice grew louder. "Yes, you, Filamena. It's too late. He won't be waiting for you."

I gave up any pretense of spying. "Liar!" I cried down to her, leaning over the bronze railing that edged the musicians' gallery. "Tell me you did not go to Angelo—"

Tullia draped herself wearily in a chair, graceful even then. "I had hoped the summer away would cure you of your childish infatuation."

"You didn't answer me," I shouted, tears stinging my eyes. "You couldn't be that cruel."

"It's enough for you to know that I did what your best interest demanded. This may be difficult, but I hope you will understand this in time." Her words were slow and considered, like honey poured into an expensive glass bowl.

"Give me my letters. He'll be there. I know he will . . ."

She shook her head. "He won't be. He doesn't love you. He told me so. Believe me, he's no different from any other man."

"I don't believe you," I sobbed.

Tullia's voice rose. "Listen to me first. Let me explain—"

"Why should I? Are you going to tell me another *fiabla*, like the one in your letter?" I wanted to be as sharp as the knife she invoked in her letter, but my voice broke.

"Which do you prefer? *Fiabla* or truth?" Tullia folded her arms. "By your silence, I assume you'd like another *fiabla*. Fine, then.

Once there were two sisters as close as a pair of doves, one with a lute, the other who sang—"

"A story full of lies!" I cut her off. "You should tell a story about a whore instead."

For a moment she said nothing, her figure below me as still as ice. When she finally spoke, her voice was barely audible. "Would you like the truth instead? It's the same as the *fiabla* but without the pretty language."

Something in my sister's tone silenced me. I wanted to escape, yet it was as if her words contained a poison that silenced my limbs. Despite myself, I waited for her to speak.

She began, her voice a flat shadow. "We did not always live here. Years ago—before you were born—I lived in another city with my widowed mother. When I was thirteen, my mother decided to ask her friend, a woman of great social rank, to sponsor me so I could be brought into society. It was my mother's hope that despite our poverty, my looks and breeding would lead to a good marriage. Because of my beauty, I was quickly noticed and, simple girl that I was, I loved the attention. I soon even believed myself in love with my lute teacher. But my mother was so watchful . . . there was nothing I could do. She would not see all her hopes and ambitions for me squandered on a poor musician."

At this, I thought I saw the ghost of a bitter smile cross her lips, but in the dimness of candlelight I couldn't be sure.

"My mother's friend introduced me to her cousin, a *grand signore* with a charming manner but the reputation of a roué. Both were so sophisticated, so *interested* in me . . . flattered by their attention, I went so far as to confide in them. Together they helped me plan to run away with my beloved. But somehow my mother discovered my plans and sent me to the country with her friend—"

"—I don't want to hear anymore." I closed my eyes, filled with a sudden foreboding. "Just give me my letters so I can go."

"Wait. Listen," Tullia insisted, her tone calm. "Without my mother to protect me, I was like a mouse among snakes. This friend knew my secret. Yet she still encouraged me, as did her *grand signore*. 'You can write your teacher a letter—we will send it to him for you,' they promised. And they gave me advice on how to describe my love, how to phrase the letter—all the things my mother never taught me.

"One evening, when I was lying in bed writing my nightly letter to my beloved, I heard a knock at my door. It was the *grand signore*. 'I heard you needed assistance with your letter,' he said. I eagerly agreed, for I trusted him . . ."

I opened my eyes. Tullia turned her face from my stare. "Filamena, I will not tell you the details, but imagine a girl of thirteen—innocent, unworldly. This was how I was when that man seduced me. When I told my mother's friend, she claimed not to believe me. Nor would my mother, who disowned me. My beloved refused to see me. Only Caterina remained loyal. Then some weeks later I discovered I was with child."

A candle flame sizzled, then died. The room was almost dark, with only two candles left—one for her and one for me. I wanted to leave. Yet I remained, my gaze fixed on Tullia's glittering hair.

"That child I carried was you, Filamena."

I watched Tullia's lips shape these words, but I did not understand them. I looked at her face so much like mine, but I did not recognize her. I felt dizzy. My hands grabbed the wall for support. "You're not my mother. I've seen our mother, you gave me her portrait—"

"Yes, you've seen *your* mother in that portrait," she interrupted. "That portrait is of me, painted when I was thirteen."

"You tell me this to confuse me, to control me, just as you always have—"

"I seek only to protect you as I should have been protected."

I was silent for several minutes, unable to think. When I finally spoke, my voice sounded harsh and distant to me. "Who is my father then?"

Tullia's hands lay clasped upon her lap, as if awaiting judgment. "Sorrow shared is sorrow multiplied. What matters is that you have a mother who loves you."

"And this is how you show your love?" I said brokenly. "By taking love from me?"

Her voice grew stronger, sharper. "As your mother, I wanted you to live as an independent woman—not as the lover of a man who can never marry you, not as the wife of one who would own your soul, nor as the illegitimate daughter of a courtesan, or even as a *virtuosa*. You can't create this life. No woman can. Only money can purchase it. If you had been patient, I would have given this to you."

Szzzzz. One candle left.

Tullia paused, as if hoping for a response. When none came, she stood up and reached into a drawer to pull out a sheaf of papers tied with thick green ribbon. She tossed them next to her lute on the table. And then she took the final candle and left the room.

I did not hesitate. I went down into the darkness and took my letters back. Yet it took some time for me to find my way back to my room; I felt as though the sea had turned to stone, the sky to fire.

Dolce waited there in front of the doves' cage, a coil of hungry intent. I ignored the cat's harsh yowl of frustration as I shoved her away with my foot and opened the door to the cage. The doves were a pale blur of feathers as they flew out the window into the night. Then I took the small portrait Tullia had given me and smashed it hard against my bedroom wall several times in rage, in

sorrow. Yet it wouldn't shatter, as if its desire to exist was stronger than my need to destroy.

In the hallway, my brown cloak awaited me next to Tullia's red damask one. As soon as I saw those two cloaks hanging there, I knew what I must do.

Just as I had when I first met Angelo, I gathered Tullia's red cloak from the hook. I wrapped it around me, tilting the hood deep over my face. Then I left the palazzo without looking back.

il risveglio

AWAKENING

MI·RISVEGLIA·LA·MANO

DEL·MIO·ADORATO

IL RISVEGLIO

I AM AWAKENED BY MY BELOVED'S HAND.

Psyche's beauty won her the admiration of many. It also won her the jealousy of Venus, goddess of love. When it was time for Psyche to wed, Venus decreed that no mortal man would be her spouse; instead, Psyche would be abandoned on a cliff where a monster would claim her.

However, Venus's son Cupid loved Psyche more than any other. In defiance of his mother, he rescued Psyche from her cliffside perch, flying with her over the sea to a distant island. There, far from Venus's vengeful reach, Cupid took Psyche as his secret bride.

MAGINE A NIGHTINGALE who had never left her cage, a girl who had never once ventured out alone into the world—a woman who had just lost all she believed to be true about those closest to her. As I ran into the night, dressed in that red cloak with only Angelo's book and letters to guide me, I was this woman.

Tullia's cloak felt heavy and strange. Stripped of the naïve ambition and hope that had imbued it the first time I wore it, it now reminded me only of its owner. I tried not to think of Tullia, of what she had just told me. I resolutely ignored her claim that Angelo no longer loved me. I clung only to the thought that he would be waiting for me.

I hurried through narrow labyrinthine streets, over bridges and along canals fetid with the smells of late summer. Everything seemed intensely vivid to me, even in the shadows and mist of early morning. The sound of the sea mingled with my shallow breath, and my shoes clipped a hollow rhythm. Once or twice I thought I heard footsteps behind me. Feverishly, I imagined they belonged to Tullia. I walked faster, ignoring the tears flooding my vision.

Just as Angelo's letter had promised, the gondola bearing his family's crest waited at the piazza. His servant did not hesitate at the sight of my sister's infamous red cloak. As he offered his hand to help me, I refused to consider what this might mean. I settled into the purple silk cushions.

Overcome by exhaustion, I dozed off to the rhythmic splashing of the gondola as it sliced through the sea. When a bird's cry startled me awake early the next morning, I spotted the outlines of an island looming before me. In the golden light of dawn, Venice seemed like some discordant dream.

Angelo's servant helped me rise from the cushions once we reached the shore. But as I stepped onto the coarse dark sand, my feet tangled in the length of Tullia's cloak and I stumbled and fell, scraping my palms against some tiny rocks. I quickly rinsed my hands in the sea, my blood a thin seam of diluted rust. I dried them on the red silk where the stain would not show.

He would be there, I told myself. He would.

#

The servant left me alone on the shore. As I looked about me, all I saw was wilderness—a tangle of sea lavender, straw-colored beach grass, cornflowers, goldenrod, yarrow and more, surrounded by rows of overgrown fig and apple trees heavy with fruit. Maddened by the sweetness, a colony of bees buzzed in concert about the coiling leaves, while black jackdaws and cream-colored gulls gazed down at me from upper boughs. Beyond stood a neglected villa, surrounded by a grove of pine trees twisted from years of steady wind.

But I did not see Angelo.

The door to the villa opened without protest. Inside, it was dark, the windows' milk-colored glass cloaked with mud. One room led to another, each filled with furniture draped in white dust cloths, like unending drifts of snow. Yet all this I hardly noticed as I frantically wove from room to room, searching for my beloved.

I went upstairs, moving silently from one chamber to the next. One room was empty but for its solid walls of mirrors. In their cold reflection, I did not recognize myself at first—my face looked strange and pale against the deep red silk of Tullia's cloak.

Holding back tears, I moved on to a room filled with trunks. A library where books were left in piles of casual disarray, precarious towers of words. A woman's room with a loom and cradle. Several bedchambers, lifeless with abandonment.

Finally I came to what I took to be Angelo's private chamber, for I noticed some sheets of paper covered with his familiar scrawl, and several books of poetry. I opened the windows, suddenly desperate for air and sun. A nest of starlings, too close to the window, warbled in surprise. The cool morning light flooded in, revealing fine bed-clothes embroidered with flowers and thorns on a rumpled bed—linens worthy of the passion of the finest courtesan and nobleman.

My chest constricted. He wasn't there. Worst of all, I could sense *her*—that lingering stench of lilies . . .

I heard soft footsteps behind me.

"*Filomela* . . . ," Angelo said, his voice rough with exhaustion. "I've been waiting for you all night."

With a cry of relief, I embraced him. The hood fell back from my eyes, sunlight pouring on my face like a benediction. Tullia's red cloak slid from my shoulders. And once again, I saw the lover's path revealed.

In the time we were apart, I had forgotten so many details of his form—the curl at his temple that wouldn't be tamed, the tiny dimple in the center of his stubborn chin, the dark intensity of his eyes. I ran my hands over his face as if burning his features

into my memory. Grabbing hold of my hands, he noticed the wounds on my palms, and kissed each in turn. His skin exuded the summery fragrance of oranges.

I heard the starlings grow silent, inhaled the scent of salt and ripe damp from outside. A cloud passed over the sun, suddenly painting the room in shadows; a few minutes later, it began to rain.

He unbraided my hair. I closed my eyes. The only sound was the singe of rain, the hollow thud of fruit falling under its relentless force.

Sometimes the language of desire is better served by absence. All I will write is that in that abandoned villa, Angelo and I were finally joined upon the lover's path. We gave way to so much more than I can find words for — passion, love, anger, grief—all things which cannot be owned by description, cannot be relived by naming.

Perhaps time has gilded the nature of my memories, but the images I hold of him now are of some bright creature—a fiery angel, if you will. I can still see his tawny hand grasping my pale one as he lay with me, my light hair entwined with his dark. I remember how serene he looked as he fell asleep next to me. How blissful and protected I felt, his arms encircling mine as I gazed out our window onto the endless sea.

But I will write no more of this now. To dwell upon our coupling is to increase a longing too great to bear.

By nightfall the rain had stopped. The following morning we awoke together for the first time. The world seemed different to me then, brilliant, crisp—everything familiar yet uncharted and brave.

"This is a dream," I whispered, staring into my beloved's drowsy eyes. "I will awaken."

"No, it is not," Angelo murmured. "See, I can touch you." He rested his cheek against my breast, his thick hair spilling like ink over my skin. "We are together. This is real."

I drew a deep breath. The starlings were now awake. He reached for me and kissed me, the feel of his beard rough against my mouth. My loose hair clung to him, as he pulled away to sit up next to me.

He looked as though he would speak, then stopped.

"Whatever you would say, speak," I coaxed, curling against his side.

He replied, "I will say only this about Tullia: how could I mistake her for you?"

"I don't want to know . . ." I began, placing a finger over his lips. Suddenly I felt vulnerable.

He took my hand away, capturing it in his. "No, I want to tell

you everything, so that you will know the truth. Your sister was waiting for me here. Her back was turned, but I knew instantly that she was not you. Water is not spirits, wine is not blood . . . I know you, Filamena. I know the way you curve your neck when you're pleased, the sound of your breath. No one else could be you."

As my beloved spoke, the knot of fear that I had carried in my chest began to unravel. I found myself staring at his mouth. Once again, I felt desire—full, overwhelming, new—awaken within me.

That first day Angelo and I explored the island together. As we tracked through over-grown woods and wandered forgotten gardens laden with sweet-smelling vines, he told me of the early summers of his childhood that he had spent there. And eventually I told him about Tullia and what she had revealed about myself, my parentage, our past.

To comfort me, he took me to the fields where he had walked as a boy. Yellow butterflies followed in our wake as we made our way through tall grass near the shore. He confided that this was where his mother had taught him to recognize the rhythm of sound by counting waves, noting their uneven but ceaseless intervals. I imagined the music I would write, inspired by our time upon this island, brought into being with him.

Later he took me bathing in the sea. As the sun began to leave the sky, I knotted my skirts about my knees. We waded into the water, ignoring the cries of the long-legged herons who protested our intrusion. Tidal pools, rich with mossy life and hidden shellfish, rushed about our bare feet—his so broad from walking, mine so thin and pale—leaving them stained with sand and seaweed. Angelo held my hand, leading me safely into deeper water where dark fish slipped by, elusive in their world separate from ours.

"When was the last time anyone lived here?" I asked. We were gazing out toward the horizon. No matter how I strained my eyes I could not see Venice. The late afternoon sky was brighter than any I'd ever seen, bluer than cornflowers.

"Years ago, long before I left on my travels," Angelo replied, a trace of melancholy in his voice as he stared out at the sea. "I was born on this island. My father brought my mother here to spare her the humiliation of my birth, but he never visited us." His face softened into a wistful smile. "My mother once told me that she gave birth to me while resting in a tree, so I would be born between heaven and earth."

"Do you think your mother was ashamed?" I asked, suddenly thinking of Tullia with an emotion I couldn't quite name.

Angelo replied, his expression serious. "She said she felt only wonder upon seeing my face for the first time."

At his words, I shivered, feeling the first touch of autumn's coolness. That night when he and I coupled, our bodies were scented with salt, with sea.

As I look back upon this time, I am touched to think of our innocence. Angelo and I were like children at play, creating our own world—a secret world where we could love; a refuge from the harsh realities of the lives we had been given.

Like savages, we gathered wild strawberries, figs, apples and olives for food. We fished and dug for shellfish. We drank sweet rainwater, found a cask of wine inside the villa that had not turned sour. We were often hungry, but our spirits were satisfied.

Mornings we spent together, rising with the sun's appearance.

Most afternoons Angelo wrote, sometimes breaking his labor to share a passage he struggled with, or took special pleasure in.

I was industrious as well. Angelo had brought me a new instrument he had found during his travels, what many now call a violin. Similar to a lute but bowed with horse hair and wood, I never grew proficient enough to play it well. But I used it to compose as I committed my songs to paper for the first time.

Often, as I worked in the light-filled library, whose towers of books we soon organized into neat rows upon dark oak shelves, Angelo would quietly join me. Silently, he would watch my hands struggle to coordinate the thin length of the bow with the elegant body of the violin. I could sense his warm breath upon my shoulder, although he would not touch me.

This silence of his energized me, waiting as it was to be filled with song—the songs I had heard in my imagination during my hours alone; new music which lay within me, like seeds hidden beneath the earth's surface.

I hold those hours in the library closest to my heart. Even now I remember the unspeakable pleasure of his quiet company. It was as if our desire for each other had crystalized into his silence, and my struggle to give voice to emotion.

The days became shorter. In the library, the sun did not linger long on the broad table where I worked.

As the weeks grew colder and the apple trees turned russet, my beloved and I prepared the villa for winter. We washed windows with rainwater, using white dust cloths for rags. We aired all the rooms and discovered a garden of flowered upholstery and tapestries hidden beneath snow-colored, bleached muslin. The terrazzo floors were rubbed with linseed oil, bringing a long-forgotten sheen to the marble surface. A supply of wood was laid in for the first frost. Angelo nimbly climbed the villa's roof to clear out the chimneys.

One morning soon after this bout of cleaning, we were startled from a heavy sleep by a loud crash. A jackdaw had flown into the mirrored room through an unblocked fireplace, and was trapped within its deceiving confines. Crazed with terror, it hurled itself over and over against the reflective walls. Long black feathers littered the white marble floor, a stark map of the bird's quest for freedom.

I watched silently from the doorway, a blanket wrapped around me, my hand pressed against my mouth. Angelo chased the jackdaw about the room, his manner soothing as he tried to stop it from destroying itself.

"I can't watch," I cried, biting my lip.

"It will grow tired," my beloved responded. "Trust me."

I cannot describe how difficult it was to wait and watch that bird struggle. Surely there is no greater pain than to watch another's distress without being able to help. But true to Angelo's word, the jackdaw gradually flew in ever smaller, tighter circles, and finally collapsed in exhaustion.

Angelo recognized his opportunity. He threw a cloth over the frightened bird and gathered it from the floor. He spoke softly, murmuring sounds that calmed me as much as they calmed the bird. The jackdaw went limp. But as he took it outside to be joined with its kind, it suddenly stabbed his thumb with its beak.

I washed Angelo's wound and wrapped a thin strip of white muslin around it. It took some time for the bleeding to slow.

Later that day as we walked along the shore, we spotted a gondola in the distance. As it approached, I recognized Tullia's boatman. He was rowing Caterina toward us.

Angelo and I looked at each other, awakened to our situation. We had tried to forget the world, to forge a life apart. But the world had not forgotten us.

96

la passione

PASSION

LA PASSIONE RENDE MENO

LA PASSIONE

DOLOROSA LA VIA PENOSA

THE PATH TO SORROW IS EASED BY PASSION.

Orpheus was taught by the sun god Apollo how to soothe the hearts of humans with song. He was blessed to love and marry Eurydice, but the gods did not bless Eurydice: she died of a serpent's bite while still a young woman. Grief-stricken, Orpheus wandered far and wide before he finally arrived at the gates of Hades. Desperate to bring Eurydice back from the dead, he descended into its depths to plead for her return. The gods, moved by the passion of his music, agreed to reunite Orpheus with his wife on one condition: he must not gaze upon her as she followed him out of Hades. But in a moment of weakness, he looked back, and so lost his beloved forever.

HIS IS THE PART OF MY *fiabla* that I have most resisted writing. Yet this is the part so many know so well. It is painful to recall the details of how happy we were, and how quickly everything changed after Caterina's visit. As I write this, I am tempted to put down my pen. But I have vowed to finish. By now I have almost come to the end of my tale, my dark tapestry nearly unfurled.

As soon as I saw Caterina, my anger and sorrow surged anew as I remembered how she had lied to me for so many years. She followed us into the villa, her full skirts trailing awkwardly in the sand, her face a stoic cipher. We walked past the great hall into a small anteroom where Angelo's father once greeted dignitaries. Angelo resolutely shut the door to the hallway, where Tullia's boatman waited for further instructions.

We sat stiffly on heavy wooden chairs, as if we were strangers to each other. Several moments passed before a table clock, newly oiled after years of neglect, struck the hour, startling me out of my confused silence.

"Why are you here?" I demanded, keeping my voice resolute.

"You are a pretty picture, Signorina, with your hair all loose," Caterina said flatly. "Here, I've brought you some food—fruit, cheese, a capon. Laura sends her regards."

I ignored the basket she proffered. "You knew Tullia was my mother," I sobbed. "How could you mislead me? All these years I thought my mother dead. I mourned her, Tullia mourned her . . ." Suddenly I could not speak.

She looked away, unwilling to meet my eyes. "It was necessary. No courtesan with a child would be admired. No future could be yours. It was for the best."

Now I was angry with a headstrong fury that only youth can create. I snapped, "The best for Tullia. She gained fame and fortune. She used me only as an excuse to do exactly as she wished."

To calm me, Angelo took my hand. "What do you want of us?" he asked quietly.

Caterina sighed, her rigid posture relaxing for the first time since she had arrived. "Signora Tullia is very ill. I would not have come otherwise."

She waited a moment for my response. When none came, she continued, "You've both been away from Venice for too long to

know how many are stricken. I am taking a risk by coming here, but I've known you since you were born, Filamena—can you really turn your back on your own mother? And you, Signore, what of your father? He is not a man easily thwarted—eventually he will bend you to his will."

"Tullia lied to me. You lied to me." I pointed at Angelo. "His father wants to use him just as Tullia used me."

The *ruffiana* shook her head. "We all make the best of what fate offers us. Sometimes the choices are cruel."

Caterina returned to Venice that same day. I could not go to the shore to see her depart. Nor did I bid her farewell. It hurt too much.

That night I dreamed of so many strange things—of Tullia, of Angelo, of the sea turning as red as fire as we sailed. Tidal currents swirled about our boat, confusing me. The starlings woke me before dawn. I reached across the bed for my beloved, but felt only empty space.

I opened my eyes.

Angelo was already awake and dressed. He sat across the room, curled over his writing table in intense concentration, the red book open before him. His hair spilled over his face, hiding his features from my view. How distant he seemed to me at that moment, under the sway of inspiration! Every so often he stopped to look out the window at something that caught his eye; he would wipe his quill on the ink-stained linen of his sleeve before resuming his labor. The only sound I heard besides the scratch of his quill was the tide, returning perhaps from some faraway land mapped in his book. I tried to think of all the places we could run to, countries whose names I knew only from his stories. Yet despite my efforts, all I heard was Caterina's voice as she told me of Tullia's illness.

As the sun rose, I watched the play of light upon Angelo's shoulder. Then I called out, "Where shall we go?"

He quickly scrawled something on a fresh sheet, blotted and folded it. Then he rose from his desk and came to me, the book still in his hand. He brushed a strand of hair back from my forehead. "You want to return to Venice," he said gently.

"Why do you say that?" I rose to abandon our bed, but he put his arms about me to halt my flight. When I would not meet his gaze, he stooped to kiss my brow.

His eyes searched my face. "Ever since Caterina told you of Tullia's illness, your thoughts have been with her."

"That's not true. Why should I care if she's sick?" I shrugged defiantly, turning away from Angelo to stare out the window. "She's probably lying."

He stroked my hair, his words as tentative as his touch. "I never saw my mother when she was so ill. I regret this even now."

My face grew hot. "Why can't they just leave us be?" I cried, moisture suddenly stinging my eyes.

Angelo held me as I wept. When I finally regained my composure, he offered me the paper in his hand without comment. It looked like a sheet of ice shearing the space between us.

On it, he had scrawled a single sentence:

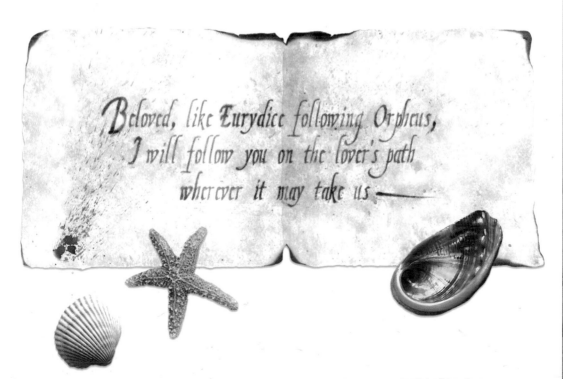

Beloved, like Eurydice following Orpheus, I will follow you on the lover's path wherever it may take us —

I looked up at him, confused.

"I know this is a small thing," Angelo explained, "but I wanted you to have my vow in writing. No matter what you decide, I will go with you. I will never leave you."

"What of your father?" I shook my head, feeling despair mingled with relief. "And what of the risk?"

"We can stand before our parents as one, or we can flee. But whatever happens, no one will part us. I swear this." And here he bent to kiss me, his lips soft and reassuring.

Yet I could not let him take me to that place where I felt safest. All I could think of was Tullia, of how benevolent and light she seemed to me when I was still a child, when I knew nothing of her lies.

Many have heard what happened that last day, though I've never spoken of it. Nor have I ever written of it before now. Yes, we did return to Venice. We would see Tullia and his father one last time, to make our peace, to openly declare ourselves before them, and to announce our intention to wed. To avoid the illness

ravaging the city, our visit would be short.

That last day there was a new fragility in the air that spoke of winter's decay rather than autumn's harvest. We covered the furniture with white muslin and gathered our few belongings. We waited until evening to leave the island, hoping the mask of darkness would enable us to travel without notice. As Angelo pushed the boat from the shore, the tide rushed against us with an eagerness that did not match my mood. He kissed me before taking the oars for the journey back to Venice. Because of the keen wind, I wore the red cloak.

As we traveled, I tried to mirror Angelo's serene expression. He seemed at peace with my decision, more so than I. I sang for him as he rowed. He beat time with the oars, matching my voice's rhythm.

Sea birds followed our path. Surrounded by water, we were a shifting island unto ourselves in the black night. I began to tremble, though I did not know if it was from cold or emotion. I stopped singing, pulled up the cloak's hood to cover my head.

Suddenly rain began to fall, sharp and icy. Undeterred, Angelo rowed on.

I tucked the red cloak tighter about my shoulders, feeling as though I would cry. "We should turn back," I said, wishing we'd never left.

"We've gone too far to turn back," he replied calmly. "I can see Venice." There it was, a floating city of shimmering marble and water, its dark silhouette visible despite the rain.

Water and sorrow . . . My throat felt tight. And the rain grew harder still. It poured off Angelo's shoulders in sheets. It splashed off my hood, pooled at our feet within the gondola. I quickly bailed as much water as I could. Somehow this action calmed me, but only for a moment; my sense of foreboding returned, stronger than ever.

Sorrow shared is sorrow multiplied . . . As we approached Venice, I heard bells chiming to mark the late hour, their brittle melody carried on the harsh wind. Confused by the fear I felt for Angelo, for myself, and for Tullia, I was quiet. Angelo was silent too as he led us down the canal, sure of himself even in the dark.

We floated past the piazza, under the bridge. A sudden flash of lightning illuminated a gold mosaic gilding a door. It guided us toward that palazzo set deep within the labyrinth of the city—that place where I had heard the sea murmur its music for so many years of my life.

As we docked in front of Tullia's palazzo, I felt as though I couldn't breathe. I cried, "We should not have come back."

Angelo ignored the rain as he tucked a stray strand of my hair back into the red hood. His eyes met mine. "I will protect you," he said simply. He wrapped the red cloak close against me. Then, stepping onto the pavement, he reached for my hands.

I know I've already written of so many things I vowed never to share, but how can I write of what happened next? I shall do so without ornamentation—no song here, only the truth.

From the shadows beneath the palazzo, a deep voice shouted, "Signora, let me assist you." A man in a gold mask stepped forward, offering a gloved hand to help me alight. I hesitated at the sight of his costume; yet it only seemed to confirm what Caterina had said about the illness raging through Venice.

"Let us be," Angelo replied, pushing him aside to reach for me. This time I did not trip in the cloak's length, but the hood slipped down over my eyes and I could not see.

"*Whore!*" the stranger bellowed, his voice oddly familiar. But before I could push the hood back, he tore me from Angelo's grasp. Now the cloak seemed to stifle my every move, its sodden folds weighing me down even as I struggled to free myself.

"Let her go," Angelo shouted, surprise and fury marking his words. "You don't know to whom you speak— "

"I know her well, Signore," the stranger snarled. "You may be the son of a cardinal, but like him, you love a whore."

Suddenly I was released—I fell to the slippery cobblestones, stunned. Ignoring the sharp pain in my arm, I quickly freed my eyes from the hood, scrambled to my feet. And then I saw Angelo lunge at the stranger, his youth and strength matched only by his rage.

I hardly recall what happened next. I felt cold rain on my face, the sharp shock of recognition: The image of a bloodied stag flashed before me, stumbling in the glistening heat of a villa's forest. I ran to Angelo, desperate to warn him—

And then I felt a dull burn in my shoulder, a tearing. I staggered and gasped. Something stained my arm, my hand. I watched, unable to move, as a dark sticky warmth ran off my frozen fingertips, spilling toward the ground.

"Run!" Angelo choked out.

I stood still, transfixed by the sight of the blood pooling at my feet. My tongue felt heavy. My legs wouldn't move.

"Don't look!" he shouted. "Go!"

Suddenly Angelo pushed me roughly aside, knocking me to the ground. And as I looked on numbly, I saw the flash of the knife blow intended for me, glinting as it buried itself in my beloved.

I remember very little after this. The sound of water rushing in the canal below, the clatter of retreating footsteps. The dull splash as Angelo stumbled on the wet cobblestones and fell twisting into the sea. I must have screamed or made some sort of noise, for others came running. Together they lifted him from sea to earth, from water to air. There we embraced, the steady hiss of sleet and wind drowning out his last words to me.

And this is where the gossip began—the stories which in time combined to become the *fiabla* about the lover's path, about which I have at last written the truth.

The gossip was wild in its variations. Some said the nightingale in the red cloak beguiled Angelo, luring him with her song to his destruction—that he fell like a fiery angel from the sky to drown in the sea. Others believed it was Tullia who wore the red cloak that seduced Angelo—and that I plotted revenge, a mortal furious with Venus for taking my own. Another rumor held that it was Angelo's father who sought to punish me, the cause of Angelo's disobedience, and by doing so killed his only son.

But it didn't matter to me what was said. I knew the truth as well as my own guilt. It was Matteo who stabbed my beloved. Upon seeing the red-cloaked figure seated in Angelo's gondola the night I fled to join him, Matteo had assumed Tullia had taken Angelo as her secret lover.

Tullia's cloak had sheathed me in the name of love. It also had betrayed me in the name of love.

Just as there are moments in life one wishes would last forever, there are also moments one longs to change, as if one could turn back the sea from its path. This, of course, is impossible.

When I next awoke, I found myself within the walls of a convent where the sisters ministered to me, murmuring like gentle doves as they undressed me and bandaged my wound. Though I immediately begged to be brought to Angelo, it took the sisters some time to reveal that he was dead. I did not believe them and insisted that they show me his body, which they had washed and lain out for his father.

I will not write of the grief I felt when they described how he had struggled for life and showed me the red cloak, stained with both our blood. At my request, they destroyed the cloak. I knew when they burned it, for the scent of oranges seeped through the convent, as if summer had unexpectedly returned to Venice.

I was quite ill after Angelo's death. Even though my blow was not mortal, I grew hot with fever and grief. I suppose I was fortunate that I was spared the far-reaching illness which took so many that year, but I did not feel thankful then.

Weeks passed; though my body healed, my sorrow did not. As I lay in bed, surrounded by frescoes of angels yellowed from candle smoke, I could think only of Angelo. Every prayer the sisters chanted to their divine spouse mirrored my yearning for him. Each time a soothing hand wiped my brow, I remembered his touch on my skin. I knew eventually I would be well enough to leave the convent. Yet I could not imagine a life without my beloved. But one day—a morning when the first snow announced winter's start—I was strong enough to sit up and gaze out the window.

That was the day that the sisters announced that I had a visitor.

Tullia was quiet as she approached my bed, her face pale and drawn above the somber colors of her gown. Her gold hair was hidden beneath a small dark cap, no doubt to avoid censure from the sisters. A large woven basket rested in her arms. As she placed it carefully on the floor, I thought I noticed a faint tremor in her hands.

"May I?" she asked, gesturing to the chair next to my bed. She waited almost timidly for my answer.

I sighed and said, "Do what you want. You will anyway." My voice felt rough from disuse.

A sudden flush arose in Tullia's cheeks. I ignored it as I turned to gaze out the window again. How peaceful the snow looked! I watched its soft whiteness blanket the world, like clean linens on a soiled bed.

Tullia and I sat silently together in this way for some time.

It was only after she left that I gave way to emotion. I wept for the sister I had lost. I wept for the mother I had gained, the father I would never know. I wept for all that could never be again.

Later that day, a sister helped me open the basket Tullia had brought me. Inside was a cage bearing two white doves, a flask of red wine, a silver chalice and a saltcellar—the same gift Angelo had sent me so long ago. It was always this moment that I remembered when my mother and I met in future years—the snow so cold and pure, her face as empty as the sky after a storm has shed its fury.

l'amore

LOVE

MI SPINGE L'AMORE

L'AMORE

IO DEVO SEGUIRLO

IT IS LOVE THAT MOVES ME. I MUST FOLLOW.

The love of Isis for her husband Osiris was as boundless as the jealousy of Set for his brother Osiris. Overcome by envy, Set killed Osiris, cutting his body into fourteen pieces. He scattered them over the earth in all four directions. But grief-stricken Isis would not let death part her from Osiris. Determined to find her spouse, she transformed herself into a dark bird and flew over land and sea searching for him. Years passed before she located every piece of her beloved. She placed each one next to the other, and, through the power of her devotion, brought him back to life for one last act of love. As they coupled, fire rose from Osiris's body, and red wings sprouted from his shoulders.

OON AFTER MY RECOVERY, I left Venice. I suppose I hoped the passage of land beneath my feet would hasten the passing of time. More likely, I sought to repair the fabric of my life in the only way I knew how: by visiting the places Angelo had written and spoken of.

With his red book as my main companion, I journeyed to countries few women ever went to alone—Spain, Albania, even Egypt. I visited distant lands where silent women wore cymbals upon their hands, kingdoms where beasts were thought wiser than men. Sometimes I disguised myself as a youth and traveled anonymously. Other times, upon my arrival in a distant city, I sang in exchange for sustenance. Over time, I grew stronger than sorrow.

It was during the course of these travels that I met you, my esteemed patroness. You gained the promise of your family's patronage, and persuaded me to return to Venice. To be honest, by then I yearned to go back, just as the sea is pulled by the moon.

As Angelo had once predicted, time and talent did reveal my songs; with your help, I became a *virtuosa*. Angelo gave me the courage and the inspiration to create music, to do what I love most with all my mother had taught me. But it was thanks to you that I was able to choose my life, unlike so many women before me. Perhaps by sharing this *fiabla* of the lover's path with you, I can at last reveal my gratitude for your many kindnesses to me and your belief in my art.

But, as I look back over all I have written for you, I am not satisfied. I feel as though I am holding a lamp in a darkened room: with my words, I can only shed light upon one small part of my beloved at a time, each a solitary aspect of who Angelo was, and all that we experienced together upon the lover's path. No words can make my beloved whole again or give full weight to memory. Nor can they really reveal what we shared so long ago, no matter how I yearn to relive it.

I am now past the age Tullia was when I left her to join him upon the lover's path—old enough to feel the increase of regret with time, to take account of my actions. I understand that things are not as simple and clear-cut as I believed when I was a girl of sixteen.

I'd also like to think I've become wise enough to see that the world is a place of wondrous complexities, of unreasonable sorrows and unbelievable triumphs—experiences that cannot be explained in a simple *fiabla*.

Yet though I have changed, some things remain: I still dream of Angelo.

In my dreams, he and I are always young and hopeful. We are immersed in the azure sea surrounding our island; he is teaching me how to swim. I hear his voice, low and encouraging, as he calls to me, as he takes my hand to lead me into deeper water. The water rushes about us as we navigate it, leading us both toward that country of desire he called the lover's path.

THIS COMPLETED FILAMENA ZIANI

FEBRUARY 8, 1543

VENICE

MUSEUM
CATALOG

Exterior, Museo di Palazzo Filomela

WHEN THE PALAZZO FILOMELA WAS OPENED as a museum in 1844, Filamena Ziani's book and personal artifacts were rediscovered by contemporary artists. John Ruskin, the eminent Victorian art critic, visited the Palazzo Filomela during an extended stay in Venice while writing *The Stones of Venice*. The opera composer Richard Wagner, who lived in the nearby Palazzi Giustinian while writing the second act of *Tristan and Isolde*, was intrigued by Ziani's mention of that story in *The Lover's Path*, as well as by the woman musician who wrote so passionately of love and loss.

So that the contents of the Museo di Palazzo Filomela may continue to inspire, what follows is a partial catalog of our many offerings.

~ M. R.

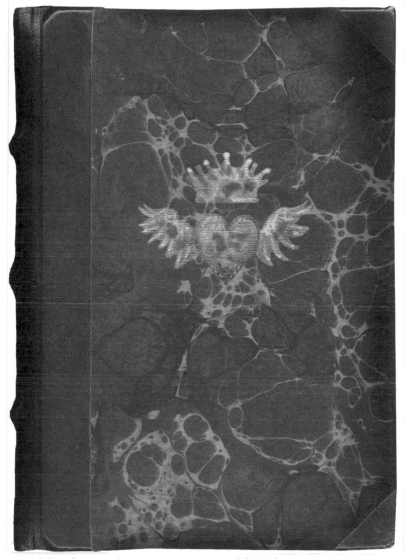

Travel journal, circa 1520, owned by Filamena Ziani.
Some of the illustrations featured within The Lover's Path
were adapted from this journal.

Portrait identified as Filamena Ziani, 1531.
Angel figure upon tapestry background is believed to be a
portrait of Angelo, Ziani's beloved.

Portrait of Tullia Ziani as Venus, 1527.
This small oil painting is a variation of the infamous Red Cloak
Venus mentioned by Filamena Ziani in La Via dell'Amante.

LEFT:
Preliminary study for
Tristan and Isolde,
La Via dell'Amante fresco
series, Palazzo Filomela.
A different composition was
used for the final fresco.

BELOW:
La Via dell'Amante
fresco series, Palazzo Filomela.
These paintings were commissioned
by Filamena Ziani in 1546.

ABOVE:

Tarot cards owned by Tullia Ziani, 16th century.

BELOW:
Excerpt, letter written in 1539 by a German traveler to Venice:
"The fashion in Venice is to brag of how one wept upon hearing the
Nightingale sing. Some believe this a sign of a pure heart."

AUTHOR'S NOTE

FILAMENA'S FICTIONAL FIABLA OF JOY AND SORROW
was woven in part from several true stories of the Italian Renaissance.
Though some of the historical circumstances surrounding women of this
era have been explained in this book's introduction, their personal stories
remain to be acknowledged.

First and foremost, the character of Tullia Ziani was inspired by Tullia
d'Aragona, one of the reigning courtesans of her day. D'Aragona was
admired for her wit, lute playing and glittering salons which attracted the
bright and powerful. Like Filamena, d'Aragona was unable to escape
the influence of sumptuary laws; to define herself as a poet, in 1547
d'Aragona published a book in Venice entitled *Dialogo della infinità
d'amore* (*Dialogue on the Infinities of Love*), which she dedicated to Cosimo
dé Medici. She also raised a daughter, Penelope, as her sister; unlike
the overprotective Tullia of *The Lover's Path*, d'Aragona encouraged her
daughter to follow her into prostitution. Upon Penelope's sudden death
at age fourteen, the poet Francesco Franchini wrote an epitaph praising
the "little girl courtesan." I am endebted to Georgina Masson's *Courtesans
of the Italian Renaissance* for bringing d'Aragona's story to my attention.

The literary tone of Filamena's confession was influenced by the letters of Laura Cereta, a woman now acknowledged as a feminist of the
Italian Renaissance. When read as a group, these letters offer a poetic
autobiography of a sensitive humanist born ahead of her time. Cereta's
letters remained unknown for the most part until they were published in
the seventeenth century under the title of *Epistolae familiares*.

Frightening violence from jealous suitors, as expressed in the story of Matteo, was a common experience for many courtesans. One story from fifteenth-century Rome relates the sad fate of Antea Sfegiata, whose sublime beauty inspired Parmiginiano to paint one of his most famous portraits. Her face was slashed by a rejected lover, permanently disfiguring her. From then on, many courtesans lived in fear of the *sfegia*, an act whose name gained fame beyond the woman who initially suffered it.

The art for *The Lover's Path* was initiated by my first visit to Italy in 1990. This encounter opened up the rich world of the Italian Renaissance for me. I also fell in love with Venice, a city as mysterious and surprising as a masked lover. Accordingly, the art and design for *The Lover's Path* is heavily influenced by the art, architecture, books and maps of fifteenth- and sixteenth-century Venice and Italy.

Numerous sources fed my imagination as I worked on the visual side of this book. Venice, an important center for the early print arts, provided me with ample material. The main book design was inspired by the *Hypnerotomachia poliphili*, one of the most beautiful books of that period. The fonts used in *The Lover's Path* were inspired by Venetian typography as well as handwriting of the Italian Renaissance. The borders for each map were painted in gouache upon handmade paper; their design was inspired by Venetian tile floors and Renaissance maps and manuscripts.

The main paintings were created with oil paint glazes, which were layered over a watercolor underpainting sealed with acrylic gel medium. These paintings were then digitally assembled into the map borders, most of whose backgrounds were adapted from the *Theatrum orbis terrarum*, an atlas of maps created in the sixteenth century by Abraham Ortelius. The woodcuts which open each chapter were taken from a series of alchemy emblems originally published within the *Hortulus hermeticus* by Daniel

Stolcius in 1627. The small color decorations that appear throughout this book were inspired by the *Rosarium philosophorum*, a series of alchemy woodcuts which appeared in the second volume of *De Alchimia opuscula complura veterum philosophorum*, published in 1550 in Frankfurt.

Many people helped me as I worked on *The Lover's Path* in its many stages and forms of development, offering editorial feedback, encouragement, and friendship. It is with gratitude that I acknowledge their generosity: Ellen Dreyer, Elise Tobin-Dyer, Sharon Glassman, Lisa Hunt, Suzy Miller, Stephanie St. Pierre, Lynne Twining and Karen Zuegner. Penelope Owen and Annelies Benke gave invaluable help with the translations featured throughout the book. My husband, Thomas Ross Miller, offered support personally and professionally; his experiences as a museum curator provided a much-needed authenticity to the Museo di Palazzo Filomela. Additional research assistance was given by the Library of Congress.

A heartfelt *molto grazie* to those who modeled so patiently for the art. They include Dale Dyer, Elise Tobin-Dyer, Sharon Glassman, Jennifer Johnson, Thomas Ross Miller, Joseph Paladino, Stephanie St. Pierre, Charles Schwartz and Christy Vaughn Schwartz.

Susan Homer, my visionary editor at Harry N. Abrams, has been the greatest champion any author could hope for. I also wish to acknowledge Stuart Kaplan and Elizabeth Kerkstra of U.S. Games Systems, who so enthusiastically and beautifully published *The Lover's Path Tarot*, in which some of the art from *The Lover's Path* also appears.

Above all, I thank Theresa Park, my superb literary agent who has the mind of a lawyer and the heart of an artist. Theresa saw where *The Lover's Path* might lead while I was still figuring out the way. I am fortunate to work with such a gifted, incisive and patient woman.

Production Manager: Jonathan Lopes

Library of Congress Cataloging-in-Publication Data has been applied for.
ISBN 0-8109-5787-6

Printed and bound in China
10 9 8 7 6 5 4 3 2 1

Harry N. Abrams, Inc.
100 Fifth Avenue, New York, NY 10011
www.abramsbooks.com

Abrams is a subsidiary of LA MARTINIÈRE

Visit The Lover's Path website at www.loverspath.com.